Old Bear

For Owen and Alison

Copyright © Jane Hissey 1986
All rights reserved

First published in 1986
Reprinted in this edition 1990 and 1991,
by Hutchinson Children's Books Ltd
An imprint of Random Century Group Ltd
20 Vauxhall Bridge Road, London SW1V 2SA

Random Century Australia Pty Ltd
20 Alfred Street, Sydney, NSW 2016

Random Century New Zealand Ltd
PO Box 40-086, Glenfield, Auckland 10

Random Century South Africa (Pty) Ltd
PO Box 337, Bergvlei 2012, South Africa

Printed in Hong Kong

Old Bear

JANE HISSEY

HUTCHINSON
London Sydney Auckland Johannesburg

I T wasn't anybody's birthday, but Bramwell
Brown had a feeling that today was going to be
a special day. He was sitting thoughtfully on the
windowsill with his friends Duck, Rabbit and
Little Bear when he suddenly remembered that
someone wasn't there who should be.

A VERY long time ago, he had seen his good
friend Old Bear being packed away in a box.
Then he was taken up a ladder, through a trap
door and into the attic. The children were being
too rough with him and he needed somewhere
safe to go for a while.

'HAS he been forgotten, do you think?' Bramwell asked his friends.

'I think he might have been,' said Rabbit.

'Well,' said Little Bear, 'isn't it time he came back down with us? The children are older now and would look after him properly. Let's go and get him!'

'What a marvellous idea!' said Bramwell. 'But how can we rescue him? It's a long way up to the attic and we haven't got a ladder.'

'We could build a tower of bricks,' suggested Little Bear.

Rabbit collected all the bricks and the others set about building the tower. It grew very tall, and Little Bear was just putting on the last brick when the tower began to wobble.

'Look out!' he cried as the whole thing came tumbling down.

'Never mind,' said Bramwell, helping Little Bear to his feet. 'We'll just have to think of something else.'

L ET'S try making *ourselves* into a tower,' said
   Duck. 'Good idea!' said Bramwell.

Little Bear climbed on top of Rabbit's head
and Rabbit hopped onto Duck's beak. They
stretched up as far as they could, but then Duck
opened his beak to say something, Rabbit
wobbled, and they all collapsed on top of
Bramwell.

'Sorry,' said Duck, 'perhaps that wasn't a very
good idea.'

'Not one of your best,' replied Bramwell from
somewhere underneath the heap.

I KNOW!' said Rabbit. 'Let's try bouncing on the bed.'

'Trust you to think of that,' said Bramwell. 'You never can resist a bit of bouncing, especially when it's not allowed.'

Rabbit climbed on to the bed and began to bounce up and down. The others joined him. They bounced higher and higher but *still* they couldn't reach the trap door in the ceiling.

DUCK began to cry. 'Oh dear,' he sobbed. 'What are we going to do now? We'll never be able to rescue Old Bear and he'll be stuck up there getting lonelier and lonelier for ever and ever.'

'We musn't give up,' said Bramwell firmly. 'Come on, Little Bear, you're good at ideas.'

But Little Bear had already noticed the plant in the corner of the room.

I'VE got it!' he cried. 'I could climb up this plant, swing from the leaves, kick the trap door open and jump in!'

In case it wobbled, Bramwell Brown, Duck and Rabbit steadied the pot. Little Bear bravely climbed up the plant until he reached the very top leaf. He took hold of it and started to swing to and fro, but he swung so hard that the leaf broke and he went crashing down. Luckily, Bramwell Brown was right underneath to catch him in his paws.

'That was a rotten idea,' said Little Bear.

'What I was thinking,' said Duck, 'was that it is a pity I can't fly very well, as I could have been quite a help.'

'Ah ha!' said Bramwell. 'That, my dear Duck, has given me a very good idea. I really think this one might work.'

IN the corner of the playroom was a little
wooden aeroplane with a propeller that went
round and round.

'We could use this plane to get to the trap
door,' said Bramwell. 'Rather dangerous, I know,
but quite honestly I can't bear to think of Old
Bear up there alone for a minute longer.'

'I'll be pilot,' said Rabbit, hopping up and
down, making aeroplane noises.

'And I'll stand on the back and push the trap
door open with my paintbrush,' said Little Bear.

'But how will you get down?' asked Duck.

'I've already thought of that,'
said Bramwell, who hadn't really
but quickly did. 'They can use
these handkerchiefs as
parachutes and we'll catch
them in a blanket.'

BRAMWELL gave Little Bear two big handkerchiefs and a torch so he could see into the attic. Then he began to wind up the propeller of the plane. Rabbit and Little Bear climbed aboard and Bramwell began the countdown: 'Five! Four! Three! Two! One! ZERO!'

They were off! The plane whizzed along the carpet and flew up into the air.

THE little plane flew beautifully and the first time they passed the trap door Little Bear was able to push the lid open with his paintbrush. Then Rabbit circled the plane again, this time very close to the hole. Little Bear grabbed the edge and with a mighty heave he pulled himself inside.

He got out his torch and looked around. The attic was very dark and quiet; full of boxes, old clothes and dust. He couldn't see Old Bear at all.

'Any bears in here?' he whispered, and stood still to listen.

From somewhere quite near he heard a muffled 'Grrrrr,' followed by, 'Did somebody say something?' Little Bear moved a few things aside and there, propped up against a cardboard box and covered in dust, was Old Bear.

LITTLE Bear jumped up and down with excitement. 'Old Bear! Old Bear! I've found Old Bear!' he shouted.

'So you have,' said Old Bear.

'Have you been lonely?' asked Little Bear.

'Quite. lonely,' said Old Bear. 'But I've been asleep a lot of the time.'

'Well,' said Little Bear kindly, 'would you like to come back to the playroom with us now?'

'That would be lovely,' replied Old Bear. 'But how will we get down?'

'Don't worry about that,' said Little Bear, 'Bramwell has thought of everything. He's given us these handkerchiefs to use as parachutes.'

G OOD old Bramwell,' said the old teddy. 'I'm
glad he didn't forget me.' Old Bear stood up
and shook the dust out of his fur and Little Bear
helped him into his parachute. They went over to
the hole in the ceiling.

'Ready,' shouted Rabbit.
'Steady,' shouted Duck.
'GO!' shouted Bramwell Brown.

The two bears leapt bravely from the hole in the
ceiling. Their handkerchief parachutes opened
out and they floated gently down … landing
safely in the blanket.

W ELCOME home, Old Bear,' said Bramwell
Brown, patting his friend on the back.
The others patted him too, just to make him feel
at home. 'It's nice to have you back,' they said.
'It's nice to *be* back,' replied Old Bear.

THAT night, when all the animals were tucked up in bed, Bramwell thought about the day's adventures and looked at the others.

Rabbit was dreaming exciting dreams about bouncing as high as an aeroplane.

Duck was dreaming that he could really fly and was rescuing bears from all sorts of high places.

Little Bear was dreaming of all the interesting things he had seen in the attic, and Old Bear was dreaming about the good times he would have now he was back with his friends.

'I *knew* it was going to be a special day,' said Bramwell Brown to himself.